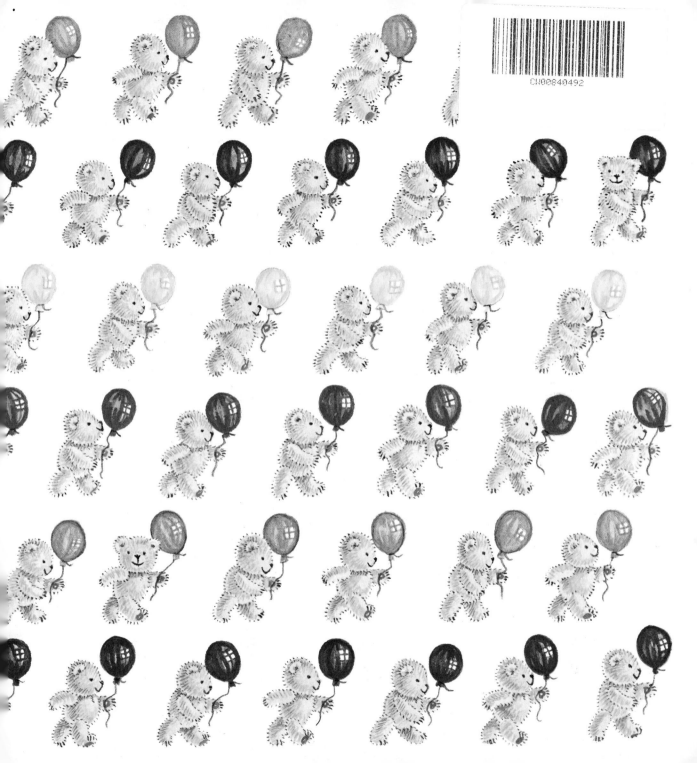

Teddy's Birthday

AMANDA DAVIDSON

COLLINS

For my Mother and in memory of
my Father whose nickname was 'Teddy'.

William Collins Sons & Co Ltd
London · Glasgow · Sydney · Auckland
Toronto · Johannesburg

First published 1985
ISBN 0 00 195829 1
Origination by Culver Graphics Litho Ltd
Printed in Italy by Imago/Sagdos

It has been raining all day.

Teddy has to stay in the front room.

"I wonder why?" says Teddy.

"Is that the postman?"

"Who are all these letters for?" asks Teddy.

"And what is that nice smell?"

"Look at all this wrapping paper."

"I can hear giggling upstairs."

"What's going on?"

Surprise!

Happy Birthday, Teddy!

"It's my birthday today!"

"These letters are all for me!"

"That nice smell was my cake baking."

"The wrapping paper was for my presents."

"And all my friends are here!"

"I *like* surprise parties."

Blow out the candles on the cake, Teddy.

How old are you today, Teddy?

It's time for some party games.

"Birthday parties are so much fun," says Teddy.

What a lovely day it's been.

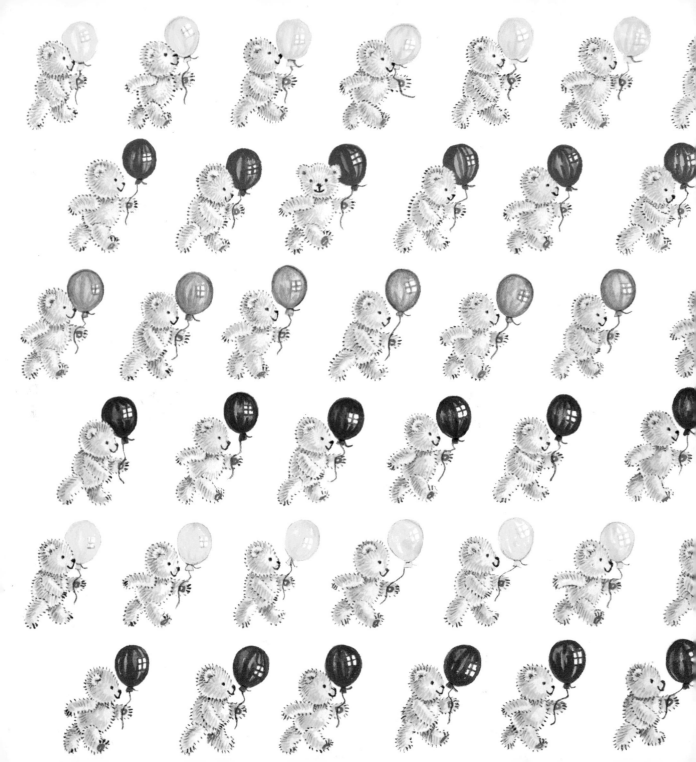